Faithfully

Faithfully

Debra Suckling

iUniverse, Inc.
Bloomington

Faithfully

iUniverse books may be ordered through booksellers or by contacting:

iUniverse
1663 Liberty Drive
Bloomington, IN 47403
www.iuniverse.com
1-800-Authors (1-800-288-4677)

Cover illustration by Mike Osborne, Gastonia, NC

ISBN: 978-1-4620-2479-7 (sc)
ISBN: 978-1-4620-2740-8 (ebk)

Printed in the United States of America

iUniverse rev. date: 05/25/2011

FAITHFULLY

My kids will tell you I'm crazy. My friends will verify I've been slightly shy of a full deck for as long as they've known me. An ex-boyfriend even told my son (several times matter of fact) that all women are nuts. That we can't help it, it's in our nature. We were born crazy. Compliments of a three day stay in a behavioral center (which I ended up enjoying), I can further on tell people—I'm certified. Not certifiable—certified! Been there, done that.

All my life I have believed in the obscure and the abstract. Must be a carryover from the seventies. But ever since I was a young girl when I started to have strange life-like dreams, like the night when I dreamt of my own grandfathers' death, I have sensed the paranormal. Some people call it deja-vu.

I believe in God. I believe in the devil. The bible reflects the fact that if you believe in one then you have to believe in the other. (This I learned personally from the time I believed in Satanism when I was a teenager.)

When I climbed back up out of that hole and mentally closed, locked and chained that door shut, I also made a promise to the other side that we would meet again at the end of days. But only God knows when that will be and what position I will hold, be it on the frontlines or behind the scenes in the battle of good and evil. (I can't dwell on this subject too long or else I'll have bad luck.)

Anyway, (I told you—they say I'm crazy.) I firmly believe in ghosts and the plan in life that we are all here as if playing in a game. A game where we're all going around trying to find our heavenly soul mate. Our "other half" shall we say. (The words of William Shakespeare's "Tomorrow" are a motto I live by.) We search through billions of other people on this planet, meeting them, having dreams about the one we search for because these are the only clues we get in the game. Hopefully, we find the right one to spend the rest of our life with. Just like in that Robin Williams' movie, when we do actually put our arms around them once again (if and when we meet back in Heaven) where we have the choice to go back and play the game of life again—if we so choose. Sometimes we have to go through Hell whether it be personal or literal to find them. But what really hurts is the not knowing if you already have found them and let them go, for one dumb reason or another.

"But when life's interrupted by dramas of her own, who lightens the heart of a clown?"

Written in my high schools' newsletter by an unknown poet.

Chapter I

Hello there! Come on up and pull up a seat. Can I get you something to drink? I understand you've come to hear a story? If you've got the time then so do I. So sit back and relax. What was that? Well, it actually all started when I was young. When a body is just so full of energy and youth. That feeling that you can do anything. A new, fresh kind of feeling that carries with you into your say, early thirties maybe, if you're lucky. Anyway, I was kinda told to tell this story but I didn't know just quite by whom until later on.

"Write it down", were the words that I suddenly heard in my mind one day. I was doing dishes in what was once my kitchen. There was a dark image just for a split second in my mind when I heard the words. A sense of familiarity stopped me in my tracks that day and I heard "Tell the story". I sat down in one of the kitchen chairs and looked up towards the ceiling, puzzled.

"Tell what story?" I said out loud. I tried to reach out with my mind and sense it again but it was gone. I couldn't even begin to understand what story was supposed to be told. You see, when I was a teenager in high school, my best friends and I would write short stories and pass them around for each other to read but that was just for fun. We were young then—it was nineteen seventy-something and the Vietnam War still seemed to have an affect on some of the teenage girls in that school.

I grew up on the south side of Pittsburgh. I was a late bloomer but I still can remember walking into the girl's bathroom and seeing two senior girls sitting on the bathroom counter. One was red-eyed, sniffling, blowing into a tissue in one hand and holding a lit cigarette in the other. Her friend was patting her shoulder and consoling her. The first girl looked at me and practically shouted, "What are you looking at?"

I was just getting ready to tell her where she could find our smoking lounge when her friend focused on me also.

"You'd be in the same shape if you'd just found out your guy was dead."

Suddenly time stopped and I didn't even have to ask. The thought came to me—Vietnam. This sudden revelation stunned me. I felt for her but my next question (that I kept to myself) was, How did she know that they would have stayed together for life? Leaving that girl's room was like coming back into modern day time. Just another regular day in my freshman year of high school.

Most of the rest of my high school days was a dance with the devil. Until the end when someone I cared about very much changed me back to what most people just accept as normal religion. But what I learned during my "black days" was that we will all one day serve a purpose far greater than what we all realize.

My dreams started when I was about thirteen years old. The first dream that I can still remember had to do with the sun shining behind a freight car of some train. There was no train station anywhere around, but it was stopped for some reason in the middle of a wide open field. A young man with blonde hair and whose face I couldn't see was sitting in the open door of the freight car and he seemed to be smiling at me. The "sight" of him warmed my heart. A shadow stood somewhat behind him. He made a comment to this other person then jumped down off the train towards me.

At this point, I awoke startled and laid there in my bed trying to imagine who the young man could have been. Fifteen minutes later, I could hear reveille being played on my parent's radio. A takeoff from the days when my father was in the army, a Pittsburgh radio station used to play it at exactly 7:00 in the morning. My father would get up early enough to get a shower for work and make it back to his bedroom in time to turn up the radio when reveille played to wake my brother and I up.

The image of my dream and the feeling of warmth and familiarity soon faded away as I readied myself for school. Only to be remembered in my senior year with a mild feeling of déjà vu. High school was not a real happy time in my life. Yet, I had found out in junior high that I could run, and I could run real fast. I could sprint like a deer and to this day, still hold the record for the 50 yard dash. But when I tried out for track in high school, the coach was not very supportive of us girls and so the idea of possibly going to the Olympics, like my grandfather wished I would do, faded away quickly also. So I met another outcast of high school life and we became very close friends. Marianne had extremely long dark hair and loved to wear a hat that closely resembled the hat that Gilligan wore in the tv series "Gilligan's Island" that was very popular in those days. She would stand outside my classroom door and pull her hair down over her eyes, set her sunglasses (which resembled John Lennon's shades) over her eyes, pull her hat down and shake her head like she was Cousin IT from the "Munsters".

I tried not to smile or laugh when I would notice her but other people in my class who knew her would see her and point her out. The teacher would then open the door to remind her that class was not over just yet, but somehow she never got in trouble for her antics.

There was also a place where us younger teenagers could go in our neighborhood that was called the rec center. It was a small, short building that housed a kitchen, small stage and dance floor which they also used to set up pool tables on during the times when they didn't have any bands playing.

It became a very popular place to be which kept the younger crowd off the streets and out of trouble. One evening, Marianne and myself decided to meet there for a night of shooting pool. A young man who had graduated from our high school two years prior also decided to come and shoot pool. Now, in my eyes, this young man was the "bomb". He had become a certified mechanic at a local car dealership. This a sign of the times that would put him above the rank of us simple average joe street mechanics. I can remember going home that first night after seeing him there and imagining what it would be like to be his girlfriend. Can you imagine my emotions when he sat with me, played pool with me and asked me to the prom with him? But still, even though we both shared a love of fast cars and drive-in movies, one day I came to the realization that he was not the man in that earlier dream and that I wasn't supposed To spend the rest of my life with him.

The night we parted ways was sorrowful. With tears in my eyes, I watched him as he drove away forever out of my life. Still thankful for him having pulled me up out of the Pit, I was once again on the side of God, but I knew I'd never see that blonde-haired, green-eyed gentle man ever again.

Chapter II

Now, mind you this was all taking place in the late seventies. I had read stories by then which were starting to enlighten me on the meaning of Life. I would go to church and listen to the men who would preach about the meaning of Life and what their views were. But what I understood was that my opinion was very different from theirs. I stopped going to church, but I still believed in God. That he placed us on this planet for a reason and I needed to figure that out for myself. Yes, the devil is after our souls. He needs them to fulfill his army for the end of days. Yes, we are all made in God's own image, but why? What is the purpose for us being here?

The seventies were a decade where people tried and smoked funny things! Make love, not war! The Five Man Electrical Band came out with the song "Signs" which made a person stop and say, "Hey! That's right!" and men would grow their hair long. Having long hair didn't mean you couldn't work just as well as the other man standing beside you. Gloria Steinem burned a bra and women followed her into a new era of Women's rights to work and wear whatever they wanted. The movie "Tommy" left an impact on me. The image of the man standing in front of the sun with arms outstretched, head hanging down lead me to believe he could have been a modern day Jesus.

Panama Red, Mexican dirtweed and whatever else was your favorite brand of "Take a trip and never leave the farm" even had an impact on my life. It started to open up my inner eye and let in some of the life that is on the other side. People started to become more open about psychics, mediums and strange paranormal events that couldn't be explained any other way. Following a new age in the signs of an afterlife, I began to have dreams about things that would happen a month, then a week, until finally just a few days later. Not knowing what they were leading up to drove me crazy. I would find out a few years later when I would be given another piece of the puzzle.

About two years after I graduated high school, I relocated to a town northwest of Pittsburgh. Thanks to my parents who were relocated to North Carolina, I ended up subletting an efficiency apartment from an alcoholic ex-boyfriend. It was a very small bedroom/living room off the back of a closed down market. It had a closet-type bathroom and the kitchen was the entrance to the place. The previous renter must have been stoned out good the day they covered the walls in a shiny gold material with padding underneath throughout the bedroom/living room. The cockroaches which found their way under the wall that divided the apartment from the old market and into the padding under this material, just loved their new home and proceeded to make it a major breeding ground. But it was shelter, a place to sleep at night for me. I had a pair of mice and I had a book on the breeding of mice. I found in said book that mice and roaches are natural enemies. At night, I turned my mice loose in the apartment. There were only a few nights until the mice got the roaches under control, where I felt first a roach run over my foot soon followed by one of the mice. Needless to say, it didn't take long before the roaches were gone.

It was here when I first had trouble with my body. I noticed arthritis settling into my elbows and upper arms from where I used to play volleyball almost every night at the park by my parents house. Never knew a person in their early twenties could experience arthritis. Didn't know then what I suspect now about a human body. Like I said before, God made man in his own image. And why is that?

It was also here that I had my first ESP dream. The one where I was at the front door of my grandparents house. The door opened and many of my relatives were gathered around talking, dressed in formal attire, getting plates of food from my grandmother's dining room table. I didn't recognize who they all were but I could sense that they were all familiar. As I wandered through the dining room looking for my grandmother a shadow appeared at my side and whispered in my ear "If you want to say good-bye to him, do it now. Because you won't be able to again."

I turned and walked back into the living room which looked now like a funeral parlor and saw my grandfather laid out in a casket against the wall. I suddenly awoke in a sweat. I sat up in bed and quickly noticed what time it was. I made myself a mental note to call my parents from work that day. It was a Friday. When I called, my mother answered the phone. Suddenly thinking I was in trouble, she sounded relieved when I explained the reason for my call. I could hear the amusement in her voice when she said to me, "It was only a dream. Don't let it get to you. You're grandfather is still alive."

The following week my father called me and said they were in town and what was I doing that night, could they come over and see me? I explained that I had laundry to do and he said they would be over afterward. Later on that evening, with my mother sitting on the couch (against the wall that had earlier had cockroaches in it's padding under the gold sheen fabric. If she had only known). My father was sitting on my only chair in the combination bedroom/living room and I was seated on my bed. He looked at me and said, "You're mother informs me that you called on Friday about a dream you had had."

In horror I looked over to my mother. Now I was going to get the lecture. Bracing myself I watched as she nodded her head.

Growing up had been very hard for me. I had once told my father that I wanted to write for a living and he had dashed my dreams. "You see all these people who want to write books or paint pictures for a living, starving on the streets with no roofs over their head and no food in their stomachs", had been his response. Now I turned my head back in my father's direction waiting for the beratement to start, he said "Tell me about it."

As I retold the story of my dream, I watched him as he laid his head back on the chair. When I was done, I sat there on my bed with tears filling my eyes, sniffling and wiping my nose on my shirt sleeve. He was quiet for a few minutes. Then I heard him sniffle as he rolled his head in my direction and said, "Your grandfather passed away."

I was totally floored and upset. Also, I had not expected this reaction. I didn't know what to say as he smiled at me and proceeded to tell me that that was why he and my mother had come up north. To make the funeral arrangements with my grandmother. Now I knew I wasn't some kind of full blown medium or psychic. But the dreams were beginning to make me wonder why they were happening so close to the actual events.

It was during this time in my life that I was doing a lot of reading of books that had to do with the paranormal. I remember a trilogy of books that really started me to thinking about JFK, our government and hidden armies that were planted in place just waiting for the end of days. I recall reading a book that mentioned a hall of souls and how each soul that leaves has to be replaced by one returning. Maybe this is where the idea of reincarnation came about. Have you ever seen the look in a newborn baby's eyes when they're first born? That look of age-old wiseness as if they've been this way so many times before. Almost as if tired even. When I saw that look for the first time in my oldest child's eyes, it startled the hell out of me. For a split second I thought I recognized the person in her eyes and had to remind myself that I had just delivered her. That there was no reason that I should be trying to figure out who I had seen there once before in her eyes. Or was there?

You see, God made man in his own image and I feel that he also did that for a real good reason. And I mean, a REAL good reason. He puts a little piece of himself in every single one of us humans, but why? If he is the largest, biggest, grandest being ever—then why would he want to put a tiny piece of himself in each one of us? I'll tell you more about that later, but for now let's continue on with the early days, shall we?

I found myself working for a place called Station Street Hotdogs. It was a combination indoor hot dog stand and separate game room with pinball machines and those large scale video games they first came out with. You know, a country singer mentions Pac Man in his song about living in the future. Well, I know what he's saying about "used to have to go down to the arcade". We were the arcade. We were the local hangout to help keep kids off the street. Kids of all ages. Now my workplace was on the hill above the town where I lived. So all I had to do was drive one street going home and the other street going to work. Both streets were one way driving through what was then my hometown.

So I was driving home from work one night. It was nice out. I think it was about mid-spring in Pennsylvania and the smell of spring was in the air. The nights were starting to moderate and I could drive home with my window open on my car. Driving down through town, the night also seemed to be a bit clearer than usual. The lights were a little bit brighter and it seemed like there were more cars parked on each side of the street than usual. I slowed down a little when I got into the heart of town and my eyes seemed to move back and forth across the road as if looking for something.

"Funny" I thought, "no reason to do this. I don't know anybody out this late."

Suddenly my eyes focused on a truck that stood out from all the other vehicles parked on the sides of the road. Almost seemed to glow all by itself. As I neared the tall standing pickup truck, I noticed that it was the color of the truck that had attracted my attention. It was a metal flake gold Ford 4x4 in immaculate shape. In the neon lights from the road, standing tall and lifted on a 6-inch lift kit, it seemed like it was a patient steed waiting for it's owner to return.

From the convenient store across the street emerged a 6 foot 4 inch tall figure of a man who glanced in my direction before jumping out into the road and striding confidently over to the driver's side door of the gold truck. He stopped for a moment and stared in my direction with his hand on the door handle as I proceeded to slow down and pass him. I looked at his face and suddenly my breath caught in my throat. My heart raced in my chest when I saw the dark brown neatly cut hair, the finely chiseled features of his face and the carefully groomed sideburns that came down both sides of his face to connect with the just as neatly groomed goatee and moustache. His eyes seemed to connect with mine just for a second before he jumped up into that beautiful truck.

Embarrassed, I quickly returned my eyes to the road and finished the drive home. Mentally and verbally, I berated myself for staring at the man whom I had never met. It was "rude" to stare, at least that was what I had been told growing up. I felt as if he was still watching me and almost raced up the outside stairs to my new apartment. Shutting the door behind me, I forced myself to relax and tried to go about following the motions to go to sleep. But his face stayed with me and I suddenly knew that I had to meet this man who seemed to me as if he were a god.

Chapter III

It was only a part-time job at the hotdog house. Counter sales, make the food, keep the peace in the adjoining game room. But it was the local hangout for young people to get together and do something. In the day and age when most public places for kids to go were suddenly vanishing, the Hot Dog House was shall we say—happening. I was twenty years old and very bored with life. So the job was like a new chapter opening in my book of life. My manager was younger than I and seemed to know everybody up "on the hill".

One night, as the playroom buzzed with activity, we stood in the little office off the main concession area, bored. Her work was basically done and I had had no one come in for food service.

"So tell me some about yourself", she said, "Where do you live?"

"I live down at the bottom of the hill", I replied.

"In Cory?"

"Yeah", I was starting to relax talking to her. I had grown up a skinny, gangly ugly duckling. When I had graduated high school, I had only really kept one good friend. Now I was talking with a girl who had probably been one of the upper crowd in school.

"Cool. Do you have a husband?"

My eyes must have flown wide open when she asked, "Huh!?"

She laughed, "Sorry. Boyfriend? Anybody?"

I shook my head, "No, not right now."

Feeling a little bit sheepish, I grinned.

"What?" she asked, "Come on, you can tell me."

"Alright. There's this guy I saw while driving home the other night."

"Yeah? And?"

"Well, I might like to find out about him."

She turned more in my direction, interested.

"Explain this," she teased.

I started to describe my drive home to her and when I got to the part where I had spotted the gold Ford 4x4, she seemed to stand a little bit straighter and her eyes rolled upward as she turned to sit down at her desk.

"Okay," was all she said turning away from me as if an idea had just come to her. I left her in her office feeling a little bit snubbed. Here I was thinking we were connecting as friends. I was confused. But it turned out to be a good thing as a customer came in at that time to make an order. When I turned around to look for her, she was on the phone. I decided to clean up the sitting area thinking at least I had told someone my secret so maybe now I could begin to move passed it and move on. After all, what would a man like him want with someone like me?

Spotting her boyfriend come in, my manager moved into the game room to visit and I walked into the back room to replenish stock. As I came out, I suddenly noticed a lifted truck parked outside the back door. Before I could look harder I heard the noise of stacked trays being tapped together on the counter. Turning around, I saw him standing there at my counter, bent over at the waist with mischief reflecting in his dark eyes. He was an Adonis!

I gulped out a hello and that was all I could get out. No "welcome to Station Street Hotdogs", no "How can I help you?". No, just "Hi"!

"What's happenin", he said, his words ran like soothing liquid down my entire body. My heart threatened to pound out of my chest. I felt like some young dumb school kid on a playground.

"Who are you?", he asked as his eyes dropped down to my nametag. I felt myself go red, silently regretting where I had placed it, and when his eyes met mine again, I returned the question.

"Michael," he answered.

I nodded my head, "Cool."

Suddenly his name was called from the game room and straightening up to his full 6'4" height he mentioned something about being back and vanished into the swarm of bodies behind the swinging double doors.

With my head swimming and my heart finally settling back down in my ribcage, I found myself smiling. I had met the man!

In the weeks that followed, Michael and his "crew" (of which there were many) were in and out quite often. He always made it a point to acknowledge me which made me feel somehow very special. I had met another man around this time who was a very laid back type of person and who also made me feel as if I were somehow worth something. His name was Mark and I don't quite remember how but Mark wound up renting the basement apartment in my own "building" which was a beautiful older house of which the landlord had made into several apartments.

Mark and I became fast friends and even if I wasn't working we would go to the Hotdog House just to hang out with the rest of the crowds. It was during one of these trips of ours that we found the gold Ford parked out back once again. Mark chose to park beside it which gave me the opportunity to thoroughly check it out. I considered myself somewhat of a back alley mechanic and was in awe of the high standing Ford. As I walked around the truck, I noticed the angry black and white duckhead custom painted on the hose of the hood. Like I said before, a six-inch lift kit added aftermarket (which in those days the state was trying to have outlawed), a white painted roll bar in the bed, and gnarly knobby tires. Just a toy—but what a nice one! It looked like fun, just—looked it.

It wasn't long before Mark started to have weekend parties at his place. Someone gave him the idea to go to the college downtown with a bunch of cars and pick up some of the coeds and bring them back to his place for these parties. It got to be known to look for us on Friday nights and several girls would already be waiting for us when we would arrive.

But first, he made sure that we didn't start anything off before I made the lasagna. It became routine. First, lasagna dinner on Friday. Second, the trips to the college for the girls later that night. Third, Saturday night—party moves to a bar called The TownHouse. Fourth, recuperate Sunday. Sometimes, we would even go to a different bar on Sunday night.

I noticed that it didn't matter where we would be. Shortly after we would arrive at our destination, Michael and his buddies would either already be there or wasn't far behind us. Now I could shoot some pool. I had been taught by a gentleman who had been in tournaments as far up as you could go. They say the people you meet, you meet for a reason. Haven't quite figured out this one just yet. But when I put that piece of the puzzle together I'm sure it will also amaze me.

Anyway, when we would go to either bar, normally I found myself already shooting pool when Michael would walk in with drink already in hand and stare at me to get my attention as he placed his quarter on the table in challenge. Normally it was Mark who I was shooting. Did he let me win so I could be the one to accept Michael's challenge? Or was it just that I was really that good? Either way, Michael and I always ended up together. At either bar, at either apartment or in my car.

I was seeing someone who was no longer making himself very available to me. He was younger than me. But when he found out that Michael was starting to come around, and that Mark seemed to be helping, he became less than nice. Arguments ensued and a very nasty fight where he spat on me and chased me in his car down the road when I went to walk away and be done with him—period!

When I went back to Mark's apartment where the party was just getting started. Mark pulled me to one side and asked what had happened. It seemed that we had been seen arguing in the parking lot. As I explained the events to Mark, the noise seemed to die down around us. (We were also changing a record on Mark's really cool stand up turntable) Suddenly I watched as Michael walked out from Mark's bedroom. He stopped and looked me dead in the eyes and said, "I guess that means your mine now."

Everything went calm inside me. The anger died and I was a new person. I smiled back at him and nodded not able to say a word. I was crouched down next to Mark. Michael went back to talking with his right-hand man and Mark turned his head sideways to look at me, smiling.

"I guess that settles it then, ain't it?" he said. Turning around to look in my eyes even better, he commented, "Gee, you got it bad, don't ya."

"Got what bad?" I asked him.

He reminded me of the certain charm that Michael and his brother had that they used when they had their eyes on females. The charm could be used in any given situation—getting what they wanted when they wanted it. Mark had become like a brother to me and it sure as hell bothered me that I had become like so many of the coeds that we picked up from the college who met the man. I knew I was head over heels for Michael and I had tried so hard for so long not to show it. I worshipped the ground he walked on and that set off warning bells in my head. I didn't want to end up a one-night stand to any man, especially this one. (I found out later that Michael wasn't going to let that happen.)

"I wish you luck", Mark said, "Don't want to see you get hurt."

It was official—I was Michael's. I really didn't know much about the man that I adored so much. But, soon I would find out just how much pull he had in the neighboring two cities.

One Sunday afternoon, Michael showed up with his brother and right-hand man with a bag of groceries at Mark's door. I had heard the knocking and started walking down the outside flight of stairs when I saw the four of them walking up the flight of stairs to my place. They stopped and Mark told me to back up and go inside. He was the first to enter my apartment. Michael had never been there and I was a little worried about the condition of my place.

"No worries. Just coming to ask you to make dinner for all of us," Mark started," Relax, they've heard about your lasagna and they want you to make it."

I looked at Mark in trepidation and he giggled.

"Where did they . . . ."

"From me, of course. It's like the icing on the cake, let's say," he told me.

Michael was standing in the doorway holding the bag of groceries. As I looked passed Mark at him, Mark turned and told him to come on in.

"You cook and we'll run. Fair enough?" Mark said turning and handing the bag to me.

"But, where are you going?" I asked sheepishly.

"We're gonna go get something. We'll be right back. Meet us at my place when it's done, okay?"

"Okay." I answered. I was young and clingy to Mark back then and I didn't like not being able to go places with him. But I trusted him and watched as they all walked back down the inside flight of stairs. Michael stopped at the bottom to let everyone out first before looking back up at me and winking when he left. With a smile on my face I knew that everything was gonna be okay and turned back to make the dinner that later I figured out was just a test for me from the man. Guess I must have passed.

I'm gonna try to tell the rest to the best of my ability in chronological order. But it all happened so long ago that you gotta give me a little error room. I'll do my best. Can I get you something to drink? Am I boring you? I kinda found it strange that this was a time in my life when I wasn't having any dreams or visions. It just felt comfortable and right when I was with Michael. I was supposed to be there. I found out that he drove truck for a living. I also found out that his mother had been married to an Italian man who pretty much owned almost all of the two neighboring towns. My car had developed an exhaust problem. I'd fix it and about two days later, it would come apart again. I would have to wait for the weekend to fix it again and in the meantime, I had started working fulltime for a trucking company that was big in the iron and steel division. So on my way to work on the days I drove through town with a loud exhaust, I noticed that when I would pass a cop on the side of the road, he would turn his head in the opposite direction. When I looked in my rearview mirror, he would be back looking in the other direction again. For the life of me, I didn't understand why he hadn't pulled me over.

I was also working tending bar on the weekends at night at the TownHouse where we would all get together. Now this bar was downstairs of one of the offices for the trucking company where I worked. So the truckers including Michael would park their rigs in the parking lot of the bar. I would start work, three hours later Michael would walk in the back door after having come in from off the road. At first, he would wait until after he had had someone pick him up and he would go home to clean up. Then after awhile he would come into the bar immediately and ask for my car to take himself home and come back. I never asked him anything, just handed over my keys. I had sold my trouble car to Mark and was now driving a 1972 Olds Cutlass convertible which was pretty quick. So I guess Michael just liked to open her up a little every now and then for me. Who knows.

Life was a party. If I wasn't working and the crowd was there with me, then Mark's apartment was the neutral meeting place. Every day, I'd turn around and surprisingly there'd be either Michael at Mark's or Mark at my door to pick me up and take us to where they were. The very first time I even touched the man was when Mark, Michael and I took a ride in Mark's mini-pickup truck. Don't remember where we were going but Michael's reassurance of "I promise to keep my hands to myself" was convincing enough for me to sit on his lap in that small Subaru Brat. I know, my heart was pounding—I think his was too!

Maybe this was the night when we were going to a party in the woods. When we reached our destination, we were walking up a path to a small fire. A radio was playing softly and a small crowd of people (including some familiar faces from the college) were gathered around with bottles in their hands.

Mark turned to me and said, "I bought you something."

He handed me a fifth of my favorite bottle of wine. He said something about it not being fair I was the designated driver all of the time. Michael wandered over our way. Seeing the bottle in my hand, he raised a plastic glass up and met my eyes with his before leaning down to say something in Mark's ear.

We were only there about twenty minutes before lights appeared on the path and a loud voice shouted something. Someone turned the radio down and the next thing I heard was the word "Freeze!" Wouldn't you know it? Here came the cops. Michael, Mark and I stood up and set our drinks down on the ground. Michael nodded his head sideways for us to follow him and we slowly started walking our way back down the path. Suddenly we were stopped and told to stay put. I leaned towards Mark and whispered in his ear, asking about what may happen. He shrugged his shoulders and said he didn't know. The next thing I remember, we were being told by one of the officers that the three of us needed to get out of there—quietly. We left the woods and moved the party over to our favorite bar.

Now once again, I will beg forgiveness for my memory being so fuzzy. But this was the time of so many parties and so many all nighters. I don't exactly remember when the gold Ford vanished. I do remember sitting with Michael one night at the bar and talking with him about it though. I had seen another truck driving down the highway in front of me late one night. It had been black with what I swore was the gold tailgate. I didn't really get an answer on that one, just a smile. Then suddenly, it dawned on me. Touching his arm and getting him to lean my way, I asked him about why the officer had let us walk away. Why the police hadn't bothered to pull me over with my loud exhaust. It all came together for me a few seconds later.

"It helps when you know the right people," was his answer. He got up and walked over to another man who had just walked in the door. I was called up to the pool table to play my quarter and when walking back from getting my favorite stick, he was sitting with this man and reached out and grabbed my leg at the thigh making a comment about "this is homegrown and cornfed. And it's all mine." I was introduced to him and to this day I can't remember his name. But he helped to protect me when Michael was on the road. I was taken care of when needed. I was a quote-unquote "married" woman.

I mentioned that when Michael came in off the road he would ask for my keys and take my car home. Then the night came that he started staying at my apartment with me. It was the next day and I was driving him home to change clothes. We pulled into the Hotdog House where he had spotted his brother driving his mother's car. Pulling up, Michael rolled down the window and his brother made a comment about me being "the wife". It made me bring up my head in wonder. Michael just looked at me, looked back at his brother and said, "Yep."

His mother even made a comment about how I was the first girl he brought home since high school. Didn't know until then just how much the man cared. Didn't figure out until way later the man had been brought up Catholic. Now in the Catholic religion, they believe in souls, spirits, the Holy Ghost. We all know that. They also spend a lot of time trying to get the general public to realize how much the Holy Ghost is everywhere! It's not just the Holy Ghost. For I have said before, if you believe in God you have to believe in the Devil. For Lucifer was God's right hand man. He was cast out and damned to Hell for all of eternity.

Yeah, we're goin' abstract here for a moment. God spoke it, Nostradamus predicted it and authors for years back have tried to tell you. There are signs everywhere. You just need to see it. There will be a gigantic battle at some point in time where we as humans all need to be ready for. Did you ever stop to think about what the long term effects of the drugs of the seventies could have. One author dabbled on this one with his story about a little girl whose parents were killed off because she could start fires with her mind. I believe that drugs were introduced to us by the Almighty himself to get us to open our minds so we could start to see the things we need to see to ready for that battle that has been written about. There were a trilogy of books written in the seventies also that has an underlying plot that if you think long enough about it, could really happen. It talks of a giant army buried undersea that will wake up and rise to fight in the battle. If the Devil can possess people, why couldn't he plant that one?

Everyday, Satan goes after souls trying to achieve the massive army he needs for the end of days. God on the other hand has given humans freewill. He expects us to return to the flock and live in peace with him when we are done in our quest to find true love and happiness. Today I watch so many episodes of the show where Dean and Sam—two brothers who fight demons to save people—and can actually place more pieces of the puzzle together that are leading up to the major, major fight that will end it all.

I read another book about a vampire who actually met up with God walking on the earth. They sat down and had a conversation together and God made comments about how he worries about how it will all end.

Many times I have been given through these outlets that God is no longer in Heaven. That he is actually walking the earth now watching today's events play out and searching. Did you ever wonder why there was such a major population explosion in the late 1900's? Think about it. Open your mind and see if you can catch the signs. In the meantime, I'll continue.

The very first time I ever rode in the cab of an eighteen wheeler was by Michael himself. I was so enthralled. It was the "neatest" thing I'd ever done. He started saying I should learn how to drive so we could drive as a team together and see the country.

21

Shortly afterward, he showed up at my door smiling, holding his denim jacket in one hand and a Harley-Davidson eagle sew-on patch in the other. I was so honored when he asked me to sew it on the back of the jacket. He played it up well and begged me to sew it on. I couldn't say no to those twinkling dark brown eyes that always melted my soul. When I finished it and handed it back to him, he hung it in the back window of the rig that he drove long haul over the road. I had passed his second test!

Now Michael hadn't really moved in to my apartment per-se. But he did refer me to other people as his "wife", remember? I found it strange though when he made the comment to me that he would marry the woman whom he got pregnant. Then he tried. That was the only time we had relations and I don't even know if he would remember. I was getting very worried with him one night because he had showed up at the bar, gotten my carkeys from me and told me he would see me "at home". Mark was at the bar that night and I got a ride home from him at closing. Two hours later, Michael showed up at my door, drunk, and I guess expecting the worse. I couldn't do it. I couldn't yell, scream or otherwise. First off, I was glad my car was back in one piece. Second, I was too glad to see him in one piece also.

The next morning I dropped him off at his mother's apartment with the words "see you later on". I had had something important to do that day and afterwards I met up with Mark and we drove back up to meet Michael and his brother. This was the only time I had a chance to meet his mother and when she found out I was there, I was ushered into the kitchen to sit with her immediately.

"So I finally get to meet you," she started.

Michael's brother was coming down the stairs and when he saw me in the kitchen with their mother, he raced back up the stairs.

"Do you know how much respect he has for you?" she asked me.

I looked at her in amazement. I didn't have time to answer.

"Well, I'll tell you. You are the first girl he's brought home to me since high school".

My eyes went bigger.

"Yeah, he holds that much for you."

Michael was coming down the stairs about that time and I don't know if he overheard any of what she was saying or not. But when he walked up to us in that kitchen I could see the humor in his eyes. He motioned for Mark and I to enter the living room with him and his mother followed.

"I'll tell you because he probably won't. Do you remember the shirt he brought you for your birthday? When he found out that no one had gotten you anything, he made sure he went out and got you something."

Michael pointed to his own chest, "I did that! I even went and picked it out myself!"

I was blown away. All I could do was smile and shake my head. His mother gave me a final wink as we all got up and headed out the door. Of course, I didn't catch on to any of this until it was too late. Not until way too much time had passed.

Michael had the rig at home that afternoon. As we all walked out to the parking lot the game plan was to meet at the bar in an hour. Michael had to ready the truck for a trip that headed out early in the morning. Mark and I had nothing better to do for the following hour so we just headed to the bar. It was always so easy to know when he arrived. It was just like Michael to make some kind of grand entrance. My favorite—open the door, step in slowly as to let the light behind you silhouette you into a shadow, pause a second (or two) then step in so the whole crowd could see it was you. Ta Da!

But I guess you could say I had my own way too. Jordache blue jeans and halter tops. I could wear anything back in those days and I had finally grown up into a woman's body and grace. Mark and I were well on our way when Michael and his bunch showed up. I wasn't quite sure if I'd heard the sound of a diesel engine or not, but when he opened the front door I knew it was him.

Something seemed to start to go wrong that day. Two many times I found him talking with another woman. A very shy girl who seemed extremely upset about something. Neither one would tell me what it was they were so secretly talking about. Michael told me not to worry about it but I still had warning bells going off in my head which I really didn't care for.

Michael started to drive long hours a lot after that. Mark hooked up with a girl from the college and drifted off into his own time. One day it seemed like I was the only one left behind—forgotten about and abandoned. Shocked, I was lost and upset the day I saw the rig sitting in the parking lot with no one around anywhere. So regrettably, I decided to write a note and follow the old proverb of "If you love something let it go free. If it returns to you it's yours forever. If it doesn't, it was never yours to begin with."

I decided to tell him how I felt in that note. That I loved him and I was going to set him free. I placed it under the wiper on the windshield of his truck and drove away. I felt as if I had let my whole life just pass me by at an early age, of what?—22? 23? I don't remember, I was just young.

I had attracted the attention of another young man who worked as a gas station attendant down the road. We started seeing each other and one day after having taken cold meds all day with no food and drinking with one of his buddys, I was stupid and let him drive me home on the back of his motorcycle. Not ¼ mile passed the bar we got into an accident. I flew over his head and landed in front of two lanes of traffic about eight car lengths forward and he fell with the bike. Gave himself a compound fracture of the left leg and I broke my nose when I hit my face on the back of his helmet, I also bruised my left kneecap.

For some unknown reason I stayed with that numbskull after that. I guess I felt sorry for him. Six weeks of doctors appointments and one cortisone shot later, I finally found myself back at the bar with him. I had parked my car in the back and as we were getting ready to leave one Saturday afternoon in the fall of that year, I spotted a familiar rig parked in the back of the opposite parking lot. Not even realizing who's it was, I simply put my keys in the ignition and was getting ready to start the car when suddenly a voice from beside me made me jump. He put his hand on the side mirror and crouched down looking me in the eyes and asked the infamous "What's happenin?"

"Nothin", I replied, my heart racing.

Then he glanced in the car and nodded his head to my companion.

"What's up." he said to my companion.

"Nothin much", he answered Michael.

"Cool," Michael nodded his head and looked back at me. Standing up he said "Never mind" and started to walk away.

"Michael," I half-shouted. He stopped and looked back.

"What did you want?" I asked.

He shook his head. "Nothin'. It's cool." and walked away. No matter how many times I called his name out, he never turned back. For years, I have been bothered by those final minutes with him. He wanted to say something. I just couldn't get him to say it. To this day—WHAT? It was nineteen-eighty something and my life was changing again. Ever hear the song "What hurts the most"?

Chapter IV

I closed another chapter in my life and moved to Ohio with my oldest child's father. For a while I could forget Michael. The beginning of my marriage was good. Once again, I thought I had found that blonde-haired man in my first dream way back when.

A year and a half after the move to Ohio, I had my oldest daughter. I was so scared at first. I never knew a person could be so inexperienced at doing something. But then suddenly you have this tiny little person in your hands needing you to survive. It took me by surprise when I first looked into her eyes. Like I've said before, what I saw in those eyes was something as old as time. Something I can only explain as wisdom.(Keeping in mind that God plants a little bit of himself in all of us.) I know it sounds strange, but that's what I saw in my newborn's eyes—age and wisdom. Now how was I supposed to raise this little being who had so much trust in my being able to care for her? I have to thank my mother for being around when my daughter was first born to help and then my very good neighbor after that. I learned fast and I learned a lot—quickly.

Two years after my daughter was born came my son. His was a pregnancy that I was told I was lucky I carried. With the cord being attached to the womb in three different places and a mass in the womb with him, he didn't have much room to grow and was under 5 pounds when he was born. He more than made up for the difficulty as soon as he was born. Talk about an eater, that was my son.

Somewhere in this timeframe the change in my husband started to slowly appear. I recall an argument (probably the one where I was pressuring him to get a real job) where the end result was a lighter being thrown at my head that hit a closet door behind me and punched a hole in the wood of that door. But he went out and got a real job. This kept us afloat for about a year and then I had to go back to work also.

I became an office manager/finance manager/title clerk/ bookkeeper for an RV dealer. I will admit that working for them felt like being involved with family and I really enjoyed working in a place where the employer had compassion for their employees. This was so very hard to find in a company in that day and age—it was the early 1990's. A time when most companys were already downsizing to stay afloat.

My husband was working two jobs. A warehouse employee by day, a carpenter subcontractor by night. He would be gone from sunup to sundown. My oldest would try to stay awake long enough at night to see her father before she would finally succumb to sleep. Our house was located in a housing development that was built in the 1950s as housing for the families of men in the armed services. While my husband was gone from home trying to make a living (at least, that's what I thought), I would make sure dinner was made for us and the venture out in the evening to visit with the neighbors. Staying on my own street of course, I became good friends with seven of the other familys. I would make my rounds visiting while the children would be on their bikes riding around or playing in each other's yards. We lived on a dead end street and everyone knew that I would be out there with the kids. The other neighbors knew they could let their kids out also and I would watch out for all of them. I loved my neighborhood and at work I was starting to be called the mayor of our neighborhood.

I developed a friendship with one young man who I could rely on as (what I refer to as) a running buddy. Kenny was too close of a friend of one of our other neighbors to be able to be an impartial confidant. He had finally found someone else in me who he could talk to and go places with. His father kept horses on a farm that was owned by this other neighbor. The farm had been family-owned at one time but the house had become uninhabitable. Therefore trips had to be made back and forth twice a day to feed and water the horses and cows that stayed there. One day I decided to go over and help. There standing at the fence was a young gray horse with black mane and tail, dapple coloring of white covered his sides and a white face to match. I was told he was a "blue appaloosa" by Kenny's father. All I knew was, I had to have Stormy. I also had to break and train Stormy. The first time we put a saddle on his back that horse didn't know what to do. He just stood there, eyes wide open, not knowing what to do next. He wasn't too hard to break but he definitely preferred me up there instead of a man. But when it came to the kids, I ranked second. Just like the time we went over to ride and decided to drop the tailgate down on the pickup truck we owned. I handed out peanut butter and jelly sandwiches to the kids sitting there on the tailgate and turned around to speak with the owner's wife who had come over with us.

Stormy had been standing next to the truck grazing and still saddled. I think it was my son who was on the very end of the tailgate nearest the horse. I was talking with my neighbor when I heard "Hey" come from my son. I looked at him. He was holding his sandwich in his left hand kind of up in the air at shoulder level. Stormy was standing beside him chewing. My oldest who was sitting at the other end of the tailgate, leaned forward to look around their friend and started to laugh.

"I never knew horses liked peanut butter and jelly", she commented. All three of them started to laugh and offer their sandwiches to my horse which he gladly accepted.

As time passed, the living conditions for my horse on that farm started to go downhill. I chose to move him to a boarding stable where I didn't have to worry about if he got fed or not on a regular basis. It was at this stable where we picked up another horse that was a professionally-trained 4H Arabian show horse. My daughter and that horse developed a bond between the two of them that no one else could share. For that matter we enrolled the two of them in a 4H group. We also decided to place our son in a little league baseball team. Unfortunately, my husband wasn't working his second job anymore and chose to join the baseball team as a line coach during the second year my son played. This made my son very uneasy as my husband was a little more strict on his own son during the practices than the other players. Needless to say, my son didn't do very well with little league.

Around this time in my life, the dreams also started to come back. Many of them having to do with the sense of someone very familiar to me. I never could see their face but I could hear their words in my head which would startle me awake. Sometimes I would even envision myself in a different house living with some other man. Perplexed when I would wake up I would remember the feelings from the dream and I would want that life instead of my own. This bothered me. One really strong dream that awoke me with a start, was the vision of a black limo being chased through the night. The limosine suddenly came to a sliding stop throwing up clouds of dust all around it, the lights of the streetlamps filtering through smoke-like plumes. One of the car's doors flew open and I heard yelling. Startled, I awoke. The feeling of sorrow was overwhelming. I didn't feel like the dream had involved Michael. But I just knew that it had to do with one of the crowd I had left behind in Pennsylvania. The thought of Mark or maybe Michael's brother came to me. But I wasn't sure. Still I couldn't help myself to take a drive back to the old hometown one weekend. I looked around in the old haunts but couldn't find anyone from the old days. It was 1990-something and I knew I had to be there. I just wasn't sure for what yet until way later in life.

Chapter V

There were a lot of nights when my husband would go fishing. He had become fast friends with a neighbor from on the other side of our deadend street. They even started going out on weekends. He would even take one of his vacation weeks and they would plan fishing trips. I didn't mind this. I had things to do myself. Life seemed good. But my husbands' personality and attitude was taking a turn for the worse. In between baseball games, riding the horses, horse shows on the weekends, work and the kids school, I couldn't see this happening. My friends saw it but kept their mouths shut out of respect for me. Life was normal—didn't every middle class family have a hectic life that took both parents in separate directions to keep a household running like ours? I still had my running buddy Kenny and the kids. Many nights Kenny would walk up to our house and just do things with kids and myself. Sometimes we would even take them bowling.

Then there came that Friday when another neighbor asked Kenny and I for help installing a new pool. I got started tearing up the ground with our rototiller and after the track got laid out for the wall, I happened to notice my husband's truck driving slowly passed the front yard. I walked around the side of the house and he stopped. Glaring at me, he watched the activity in the back yard while I approached the truck.

"Hi," I said as I reached his side window, "You're home early."

"Yeah. They told us to leave since we were done with work. What's going on here?"

"Just helping put up a pool", I answered him.

"I see Kenny's with you."

"Yeah. Along with about ten other people," I informed him.

He tried to look passed me at the group of people who were starting to form around the work area. Suddenly the man who owned the house came out from the front door and walked up to the truck.

"Hello", he said to my husband, "Coming over to help too?"

My husband smiled at him and said, "Thinkin' about it. Let me take the truck on home and I'll be down."

"Okay," my neighbor answered and walked away.

Right about then he spotted the rototiller.

"Is that my rototiller?" he asked.

"Yeah. I brought it down to make the spot for the pool."

He gave me a look that told me he was none to happy about that.

"Are you done with it?"

His attitude with me was always different than what he showed to anyone else. My dead sister-in-law had made it a point to inform me of that.

"I think so," I answered.

"Get it home!"

"All right," I replied just as he started to drive the truck away.

As I walked the rototiller back up the three houses home, all I could think of was—Lord, why did you have to bring him home early today of all days?

He was backing the truck in the driveway when I walked in the front yard with the tiller. I chose to leave it there until I returned later from finishing the rest of the pool. My husband climbed down from his truck and asked if I was coming in the house with him. I replied "no" that I was going back down to what I was doing and returned to our neighbor's house. Shortly after, my husband was there wearing his tool belt and carrying his electric drill. I started to relax thinking maybe his attitude would change now that he was going to be doing something amongst a good bunch of people and he would enjoy himself. I knew he got along with Kenny—they even went fishing together sometimes and working outside always made him feel better.

We were all spread out along the pool wall holding it in place. My husband and I were at the seam since we had done this before. He asked me to hold it together while he started the screws that held it in place. Over the sound of the drill I never heard him say a word to me. Then he yelled something. Still holding the top of the wall together, I turned my head to look at him. He lost his temper at that point, smacked my hand down onto the top of the pool wall and yelled, "I said you can let go of it!"

Now everyone who has dealt with either building a pool or sheet metal or aluminum knows that these edges are very sharp, period. I jerked my hand back and immediately saw blood. I grabbed my hand and bolted towards the house. My neighbor's wife was just coming through their back door when she saw me coming and took me to their bathroom. Her two boys were right behind her. I showed her my finger and she immediately grabbed a washrag and soaked it in cold water.

At the same time she started to chase her boys away from the sight of my hand. Not knowing, her sons ran out of the house yelling for people to start looking for the top of my finger.

"How bad is it?" I asked her.

"You need stitches," was her reply.

Her husband suddenly appeared in the doorway and she informed him to go get my husband to take me to the emergency room. The top of my finger was still attached to my hand but barely. When my husband walked in he seemed oblivious to what he had done. Something I sensed he was faking since I know he knew how sharp pool walls are. I was shocked. But then again, I had recently heard from another neighbor about a discussion the two men had had about what they were doing for their wives for Mother's Day that year. My husband had told this neighbor, "Nothing. She's not worth it."

Now, I was starting to realize that our marriage was in real trouble. It was probably over. Just two people residing in the same house for the sake of raising two children. The only thing we were holding onto was obligation. I would spend my mornings after this sitting at the kitchen table, drinking my coffee before waking the kids up for school, crying, wondering, "Is there life out there?" Then came the days when he would come home and threaten, "If things don't change around here, there's the door!" Our son would come home from school and would be sitting on the living room floor watching tv right up until the time his father would pull in the driveway. Hearing the truck, he'd get up, look out the front window, shut off the tv and bolt out the front door shouting "Bye mom."

I knew we had to do something. Then the dreams started to really come back. The dream having to do with a stranger and a different house. It was a house that I didn't recognize being owned by anyone I already knew but felt like I belonged there. I awoke in the morning quite puzzled about where this house was and who the man could be that felt so comfortable to me. I was stuck in a life that had no resemblance of my dream for the rest of my days.

The next dream to come to me was more like looking into darkness. But I knew it was him. The quick glimpse of his outline and the sheer familiarity of him standing behind me, his voice in my head—Michael. I guess you might not call it a dream. More like a nighttime meeting of two souls when your subconscious is wide open. I walked around for a week in a daze. Wondering why now? Did I need to go back again but this time—find him and see how he was doing? It made me realize that my love for Michael was still strong enough to outweigh the love I had ever felt for my husband and that was sad. The words of the song "Separate Ways" could not have described my outlook any better than then.

Then came the day that prompted me to tell this story. The bright, sunny afternoon when I was standing in my kitchen, my husband at work, my children at school and I was washing the dishes. All of a sudden inside my head I saw that all too familiar black shadow lean towards my left side and the voice telling me to "Write it down!". I stopped dead in my motions. "Tell the story." Then the vision was gone leaving me once again dazed and confused. I won't go retelling my actions after that. I already related that one at the beginning of my story. What I didn't tell you was that somehow I sensed that I was to tell the story about him. But I didn't know why (once again) until years later. I wasn't to know for many years what these words were to mean. I think now I do but I can't tell you just yet. I have to finish the story.

It was about the late 1990s and as per my doctor I had to leave the RV dealer were the stress of the job was giving me panic attacks. He was afraid these would lead to something more serious. So I took on an assistant manager position at a local lounge which none the less only aggravated my marriage. My husband wasn't at all happy with my decision. But he didn't mind the money that I brought home every day. All of a sudden it felt like I was the main money maker in the house and this didn't please him very well either. I worked weekends then had a few days off before having to return back to the work. It seemed like his anger would become more volatile towards the middle of the week and finally blow off on the weekend while I was at work. This was not a very good situation for my children to be in.

I developed my own crowd of regulars that would come in to the bar on nights that I would work. Several of my regulars started to notice a slight difference in my attention. When I was asked about what I would be thinking about, I suddenly found myself telling them some of what was happening on the home front. A few of these regulars, mainly two men and one woman, started to pay close attention to my situation. One of these men was very young (just turned 21) yet seemed to have a level head on his shoulders. Well, except for the fact that he had lost his license to DUI charges. Rather than have the young man's mother or father wake up at 2 am to come pick their son up from the bar at closing time (they both had to get up early the next day to go to work), I elected to drop the young man off at home on my drive home from work. We became friends and I found myself really relying on him as my sounding board about my life at home. Not only did I have Shawn really concerned about the "domestic violence" that was going on in my house, something I wasn't seeing myself, but the other two regulars were telling me to get out before it became too bad to handle. I was also by this time seeing a psychic. She had informed me that my dead mother-in-law "hated you in life, hates you more in death". The psychic also informed me that my husband's hot and cold attitudes had to do with his being involved with someone else.

The first incident on my children from their father, I witnessed myself. He had come home from work and was sitting at the kitchen table with me. I don't remember the entire conversation. What I do remember was him removing his watch and throwing it into the living room where the children were watching tv, just missing their heads by inches. I do remember his infamous saying of "There's the door!" and a new comment came out of his mouth of "I knew it would be trouble when I couldn't keep you at the RV dealer". But what shocked him was that by this time I had already used his own words against him. You should have seen the look on his face when I told him—"There's the door!"

The second incident was about a month later. By this time I would come home from work at night and crawl into bed with our daughter. (She had a queen-sized waterbed). I guess I was starting to put two and two together by this time and was wondering how in the world I was going to leave the house with two children and survive. I really just wanted him to leave. He had family nearby. My parents had divorced by this time—my mother was living in Florida and my father was in Nevada. I had nowhere to go.

Anyway, it was summertime and the next morning the kids woke me up and my son proceeded to inform me that his daddy had gotten mad at his sister the night before and had thrown a wooden kitchen chair which had hit my daughter in the leg. My daughter tried to tell me it was a plastic lawn chair but when I inspected both her legs I found bruises which told me the chair was harder that a lawn chair. Now by this time, Shawn and I were talking on the phone together. When he called me later on that day to check up on us, he told me if I didn't call the police soon then he would. I new I needed to do something quick. I was really shell shocked. Had my marriage really come down to this? This was the story you saw on the nightly news on tv. This was happening in my house! The other male regular told me I had to make a choice. Quit my current job, stay at home and try to work it out with him in which case it might get better, or call the police, file a restraining order on him and file for divorce. I didn't know what to do, I was scared to death. I didn't have much time to think about it however. About three weeks later, the third and final incident occurred.

Once again, while I was at work, my daughter had been playing at a friend's house two doors down from ours. She had been swimming and when asked if she could spend the night there, she had rushed home to ask her father. Still somewhat damp from the pool she entered the house through the living room front door and found her father on the phone, crying. She told me that she thought he was talking to me as he told the person on the other end that he loved them and hung up quickly when she entered. Then he turned on her.

"What do you want?" he asked her.

When she asked if she could spend the night out, he agreed. Exuberantly like all children at about age ten or eleven do, she through herself at him to give him a big hug in thanks. He reacted by half-punching half-shoving her in the stomach with a force that made her feel sick to her stomach.

"Now get out of my face," he told her which also upset her.

Looking at her friend who had come home with her she turned and left the house. The next day when I was informed of this latest threat to my daughter, I called my new confidant and he advised me once again that if I didn't call the police, then he would for sure this time. This was child abuse! So I made a phone call and arrangements for my daughter to speak her story with a detective after which the children and I got out of that house until something could be resolved.

A few months later found me living in a small efficiency apartment once again. Only this time sharing it with my new best friend Shawn. I had the bedroom with a king-sized waterbed and he had the living room/kitchen with a hide-a-bed couch. The detective on my case had determined that the problem with my husband and the children was being instigated by me being in the house. He felt that if I left, the children would be safe staying in the house with their father. Since school was soon starting, I decided to try this so their school would remain the stable point in their life. It seemed to work out to begin with but then came the Sunday when my son called me at Shawn's parents house asking to come live with me. It seems that when Shawn and I had dropped the children at their father's house, he had drilled them for information on the sleeping arrangements in my apartment. The night beforehand I had closed the bar downstairs and Shawn had put the children to bed earlier in the night in my room. This was a new job for me also so when I walked up the stairs when I closed the bar, Shawn wanted to hear about how the night had gone at work. We talked into the wee hours of the morning and both had fallen asleep on his hide-a-bed fully dressed.

When the children woke up the next morning, they came bouncing out of my room and woke us up. When it came time to take the children home, I guess both my soon-to-be ex-husband and my daughter had teased my son about being a mama's boy. My daughter was very close to her father and my son basically feared his dad. So he called me to come live with me. When I went back to pick him up, all hell started to break loose. I was approached by my husband who threatened my son with my death. As I told my son to get into the car, I looked at him and asked him what his problem was. It seemed that when he questioned the children about the arrangements at the tiny apartment, all he heard were the words mommy and Shawn slept together. As his anger rose, I calmly looked at him and said, "I'm not going to talk with you about this until you've had a chance to calm down."

I turned to walk to the car and a small one-sized cereal box flew passed my head and fell short of hitting the front end of the Toyota. Later on he told the children that he wished it had been a rock. I just kept walking and never turned back.

That incident still got to me though. My heart was pounding in my chest. My son had raced back into the house to call 9-1-1 but my daughter had stopped him as she knew there would have been an arrest on that day. It was within six months after the original charge had been filed against him. I simply went back to the bar where I was currently working, downstairs of where I lived, and the owner there when he heard my story and saw the tears rolling down my face, told me "It's your bar. Go get yourself a double of whatever you want." I got shit-faced. If my youngest daughter ever reads or hears this part of the story, she'll lose it. She will want to commit me. But when her father (Shawn) chose to take advantage of the drunken older woman (he was plastered also, this was not normally part of his nature). Afterward, as I lay in bed, I heard a voice that told me—"Now you're pregnant."

Oh so true. Yes, I was. So here came child number three. I decided to try and make a go of it with Shawn which in the end didn't go so well either.

Chapter VI

Now I told you I'm crazy. I even had picked up my own set of tarot cards and I could read them for anybody else. But for myself, it can't be done! The dreams were really starting to once again lead me into my future. By this time they didn't startle me though. I had accepted the fact that a part of me was something special. Everyone has it, not everyone accepts it. But God hid it in us. Sometimes, it becomes so big that our bodies can't even hold it. That's why some people experience disabling issues with our bodies. Because of that little piece of Him that we all hold in ourselves. Too much for now? Then I'll go on.

Remember that dream I mentioned about being in a strange house with some strange man I'd never met before? Well guess what, it became reality after I had my third child's father move back into his mother's house.

He was a little older than myself, tall and lean, and another clown. In my foreward I posted a saying I read in my high school newsletter. My answer is—another clown. When I met this man, he told me "I'm certifiable" and my response to him was "Ha! I'm certified! I have my papers." He laughed at me and said, "I admire that. All women are crazy, they can't help it. They're born with something that makes them that way. At least, you're willing to admit it."

In the following weeks, I grew very fond of him. He had a sense of humor that kept me laughing and buoyant. He even actually seemed to have a heart. He showed me what it was like to be gentle, because he was. He showed me what it would have been like to have grown up in a loving, caring household. Firm yet—loving. He could accept difficulties and work through them. On a Friday, I received a phone call from him.

"What are you doing later?"

"I don't know, why?"

"Because I need a woman's opinion. My son and I need to go shopping."

Chuckling I asked, "What for?

"We need to go to a funeral in New York this weekend."

"Oh no, I'm sorry. Who died?"

"My mother-in-law."

"Okay."

"You know what they say, you can't divorce your in-laws."

"I know," I responded. My thoughts were going fearful. Distrustful after all I had been through, I started to think about what might happen if he got back together with his ex-wife under those circumstances. Trying not to let it get to me, I agreed to meet him later that evening for dinner and shopping. He had been married twice before and the first time was to a Seneca Indian half-breed whom he had met in high school. He had had trouble with her straying around with other men all through school and it had bled over into their marriage. Still, he tried to make it work for the sake of their son. Finally, one day he just had enough and packed everything he could into his truck and left. He had told me that even though their marriage hadn't lasted he could still get along with her afterward. It had just been the infidelity that had broke up their marriage. They still had remained friends.

His mother-in-law at some point in time moved back up to the Indian reservation in New York. He had always gotten along with her and when he was told of her passing, he was going to make it there to say his goodbyes no matter what. He had loved his mother-in-law as if she were his own mother who had died of cancer five years prior.

The weekend after shopping for suits for himself and his son was spent cleaning and detailing his car for the trip to the funeral. It was a beautiful bright sunny September day. After his son washed the car, the man was waxing it and I was stretched across the back seat on my stomach talking to him. With my heart pounding in my throat, I decided to ask him about my fears in regards to him and his ex-wife.

He looked at me with his sharp brown eyes that were also gentle at the same time. He started to smile, "Someone getting attached, are they?"

"Maybe a little," I answered just a little embarrassed.

"That's okay. But let me assure you, there's nothing to worry about."

"But what if . . . .," I started.

"Stop! There's a reason she's called an "ex" wife. Understand?"

All I could say was okay. I had butterflies in my stomach and I just wanted to run away about this point. I was afraid I had taken it a little too far with him. As we continued talking that afternoon, I finally really started to understand him. He was the type of person who would try to work out any obstacle to keep hold of what he wanted in his life. When I went home that evening, I sat back and asked myself if he could hold a candle to Michael. He was starting out on a good note and only time would tell. He was definitely different from other men. Something he had already informed me of himself.

Tuesday of the following week I was starting my day as usual. I had gotten up and sent my older two children off to school. I was getting ready to go visit my friend who was the manager at a local tobacco store when something attracted my attention to the tv. Staring at the tv set, I wondered what the name of the movie was that would have been a drama type on television that early in the morning. Then, in disbelief, it occurred to me that it wasn't any movie. Enraptured in the tv, I watched while smoke billowed from a tall skyscraper while an airplane circled around it's twin and the flew directly into the second tower. I almost jumped straight up off the edge of the couch when I realized I was watching the scene unfold from New York. The date was September 11, 2001.

I started to listen to the newscaster and the sound of people shouting. It was terrorists that were attacking the United States. I looked over at my youngest daughter playing in the living room and was filled with panic. What was life going to be like for us now? As I heard about other attacks on other parts of the country I slowly sat back down on the corner of my couch and watched while the two towers burned and collapsed on television. I began to wonder if it was the beginning of the end. Was that why I had dreams? Was I to get ready for the battle at the end of days? What about my children? Suddenly I wanted to get to my friend because I needed some kind of moral support on how to handle this, I guess. When my daughter and I arrived at the cigarette store we did our usual hellos and she assured me that the attacks were not the beginning of the end. Then she asked me about my new boyfriend. As I told her that he was on his way to New York for a funeral, it finally clicked in my head where the towers were and where he was going.

I looked at her in surprise, "I'd better call him."

"I guess you should," she answered me chuckling.

Somewhat alarmed I picked up my cell phone and dialed his number. He didn't answer the first time. As we discussed where in New York he was going, I could feel myself becoming more anxious.

"You really like this guy, don't you?" she asked

"He is probably the best thing that's happened to me in a long time," I replied, "and I have such a good time when I'm with him. I guess I just don't want to lose him just yet."

His son finally answered the phone and informed me they were still on their way to the reservation. He finally got on the phone.

"Hey," he said.

"Hey," I responded, "Where are you in New York?"

He informed me that they had gone passed New York City hours beforehand and were not aware of what had happened behind them because the radio didn't work well in the car. Relaxing, I told him that maybe he should try the radio and listen in on what devastation was hitting our country. I was relieved to know that the newest enjoyment in my life would be back home in a couple of days.

Those couple of days led to six years. I had made mention of the fact that I was ready to reach out for and grab hold of the infamous brass ring. He told me that he couldn't promise anything but he would try and help me get it. My thoughts one day went to the same questions when I meet someone. Was this the one that would help me forget Michael? Being under Michael's protection when I was younger, if he ever called me and asked me for a favor could I see him again and know I wouldn't be right back in love with him again? Could I love someone just as much as I did him if not more? Would the next one I became involved with be the one that would outweigh my feelings for a man so long gone? Or was Michael the one that I should have spent the rest of my life with?

When my newfound love came to me one day about three months after we first got together with the idea of looking at houses, I once again became afraid that I could lose contact with him. Not his idea however. He informed me as we sat riding in his car to look around that he had been looking to buy a house for himself and his youngest son. Now we were going to look for a house for a larger family if I was willing to combine efforts and move my family in with his. I didn't think I could contain my excitement. But I guess I played it off pretty well. I weighed it over in my mind and informed him that I would. I can't explain the feeling I got after we moved into the house that we found.

Mind you, it took six weeks just to clean it out to move into. It was an estate sale and the family had left so much old memorabilia in the crawlspaces. They just abandoned everything and anything in the basement. The huge backyard needed old doghouses and chicken coops removed. An old falling down barn needed to be knocked down, torn apart and burned. Every room needed something done in it. With my new other half working 12 to 14 hour days, it was up to me to get things done. In my younger days this would not have been a problem. But I was getting older and my stamina just wasn't with me anymore. Especially when I was working alone. I would start out strong in the morning, go over to the house, make a decision on what I wanted to accomplish that day and get started. By mid-afternoon for some reason, I would want a break. This would sometimes lead to a siesta. Then by evening all I wanted to do was set my mind on food. So he would get off work, drive to the house to pick me up and we'd go get dinner. By then it was too late to go back and start unless it was a weekend.

Now the strangest things started to happen. At first, it was just odd phone calls. When you entered the house from the front door, you entered the living room. At the other end of the living room was an arched doorway of which on the other side of the wall about halfway up was a wooden insert which used to be a phone ledge(?) at the bottom of the stairs which led to the second floor. Now the phone line coming into the house ran through the walls and down to an outlet on the other side of said wall and mounted on the baseboard in the living room. This house was built circa 1950. Of which, there would have been a party line for phone service at that time. Now, I would be alone in the house. It would get to be about 4:20 in the afternoon when all of a sudden I could hear a phone start to ring in the living room. Now my male companion had already turned phone service on in the house in his name. I would answer the phone expecting it to be him. Sometimes it would be but I could hear static and faint voices around his voice. Now there are no more party lines in that area of Ohio anymore. Just regular dedicated lines. After several times of answering and talking to no one, I eventually stopped answering it when it rang at that time. I would still shout out "hello" into the air though when I would hear it ring. One day I noticed that it had gotten to be about 4:30 and the phone hadn't rung yet. Five minutes later, it rang. I lifted my hand into the air and said, "You're late." It immediately stopped ringing. But the next day the phone rang at 4:20 again. Eventually it did finally stop altogether though. Once we moved in with everyone and settled down to continue on with life.

Now my friend would sometimes notice the smell of a cigar in the air. We both smoked cigarettes and didn't know where the cigar odor would come from. Also, there were the times when tools would suddenly end up missing and you would find them somewhere else anywhere from thirty minutes to three days later.

One day after the hot water tank let go. He was working in installing a new one in the basement while I painted upstairs. Deciding to take a break, I walked halfway down the stairs holding a bottle of beer in one hand for him and a glass of wine in the other for me. Sitting on the step, I handed him the beer and we "took five". After discussing our game plan, I went back up to work in the room I was in, he set the beer down on top of the hot water tank and went outside to the garage to locate a tool that he needed to finish. I heard him come back inside and go down in to the basement. After a few minutes I heard him yell up to me.

"Hey babe."

"What."

"Did you take my beer up there with you?"

"No."

"Did you see where I left it?"

"You set it down on top of the hot water heater."

"That's what I thought, but it ain't there now."

To this day we still don't know where that bottle of beer went. Never did find it. I knew what was going on. He didn't want to believe what was going on. The previous owner also loved children. This was substantiated the following spring when I let my youngest out the back door to play. I was (once again) washing dishes in the kitchen with the back door open so I could hear her. She came in, got a ball and went back outside. I didn't think anything of it. I could hear her laughing and talking outside and wondered if the neighbor boy had come over to play. I walked over to the door and looked outside. I only saw her. Calling her in I asked her who she was playing with. She told me that an old man wearing a flannel shirt and blue jeans was outside with her. When I spoke with the neighbor they informed me that I had described the man who had previously owned the house.

Not only did we have the previous owner's presence in that house but we lost my companion's father that spring and suddenly it felt as if there were three spirits around playing games with us. His mother was also around him. I remember laying in bed one night with him asleep beside me and I could hear his breathing starting to become congested. As I lay there in the dark I watched two small dots of light bouncing up and down making their way across the closet door. As soon as the lights reached the end of the door closest to my boyfriend, he started choking in his sleep and raised himself up on his arm into as much of an upright position as he could. He rolled himself into a sitting position and looked backward over his shoulder to me.

"What brought that on?" he asked bewildered.

I was wondering," I said.

Shaking his head, he lay back down and wiped his forehead, "I was having the strangest dream."

"About what?"

He proceeded to tell me about one of his parents (I think it was his mother) being in his dream. I started to smile and when he looked at me funny I told him about the moving spots of light on the bedroom closet door. He gave me a look and rolled back over onto his side.

"They can let me sleep, I gotta get up early in the morning and go to work."

There were quite a few times that they made their presence known. But I learned to live with it. Not so with him, every time they would decide to play games with him, he would shout out "Get out of here! This is my house now!"

Yes, spirits are becoming more and more known. There are reality shows which have come out that proves to us they are around us everywhere. Anybody wonder, why now?

It was this spring that I also put my back out for the first time. We had gotten back from his father's viewing and it was late. I was dressed in high heels and was trying to lift my sleeping child up from out of the back seat of his car when suddenly I couldn't move. I couldn't straighten up. He had to take her from me and then help me into the house. With physical therapy I recovered from that one very well. But what was going on with my otherwise healthy body?

A few years later I was working for an auto parts store. One of the bigger chains that you find advertised all the time on the radio and tv. It was around December that year that I decided to work as much as I could to finance a trip on a cruise line for his Christmas present as he had never been on vacation before. At the end of my three weeks straight of working without a break, I woke up tired on the last day and was fighting to wake up and ready myself for work. I was sitting at the kitchen table drinking coffee when all of a sudden I was hit by an allergy attack. One of those that start you coughing and you can't stop. I found myself wanting to sit up as straight as I could and when I did, I jammed that weakened disc out in my lower back. There was pain there that I hadn't felt the first time. This pain ran down the outside of my left leg to my calf. It wasn't really what you would call pain though, it was the feeling of electrical needles stabbing. I'd done it good this time and it was a Sunday. Jumping back into bed I called work and called off. The next day I phoned my doctor's office and was told the closest appointment was the following Friday—over a week away. I also found that sitting on couches was going to be impossible. So my boyfriend's youngest son brought out a type of foam cushion that I could lay on in the living room. I spent most of my time on that cushion. But that Thursday night as I lay there after everyone else had gone to bed. I felt that I needed to go to the bathroom. As I sat on the royal throne, I started to cough again. I coughed so hard that I jammed the disc again and sent fire down into my toes. I jumped up off the toilet seat screaming and my left leg gave way underneath me. I wasn't used to pain. I lay there yelling and writhing. Now here I am, half naked on the floor and who gets to me first. Wouldn't you know it, his youngest son. Of course since his bedroom is the one directly under the bathroom in the basement. Right behind him was my boyfriend who got the idea real fast to cover my body with my robe.

I was in so much pain—pain like I had never ever felt before. I knew that their was an ambulance ride in my so very near future. When the arrived and loaded me into the ambulance, it was everything I could do to keep from screaming out in pain with every bump. My boyfriend's youngest son followed behind as he wasn't working at the time so it was the smartest option for him to be my ride home if warranted.

Now remember when I said that God plants a little piece of himself in all us humans. He is so grand and has such longevity that our mortal bodies can only hold so much for so long. He made us in his own image yet he also made us that our bodies would only hold out for so long that when new younger bodies came along, he could replant that one piece we hold in our body into a newer one. Make sense yet? As our body grows older, it becomes weaker. We all know this. Even a country singer came out with a song that mentions not being as good as he once was.

I spent three days on a liquid morphine drip so I could get sleep and hopefully relieve some of the pain. As long as I stayed in bed I felt no pain but every time I went to get up and walk, I felt the fire run right back down into my foot. My left side was affected. My job at the auto parts store was put on hold until after five months I told them to release it. Physical therapy was not working this time and in August of that year—2004—I had to have surgery to remove the disc fragment that fell under the nerve stems and was cutting into them. I now have permanent nerve damage in my back complicated with arthritis that will not allow me to work a full time job. I spent many of those Ohio winter days doing nothing but laying down. My boyfriend was afraid to touch me in an intimate manner. I couldn't blame him, he didn't want to cause me any more pain. I started taking three different kinds of pills three to four times a day to help me handle the pain that was constantly with me no matter what. The only relief I had was when I woke up in the morning before I would make any move. Sometimes I would just lay there for five minutes to remember what it was like to have no pain in my body at all.

Besides the reality shows about ghosts I also started watching a brand new tv show that came on on Thursday nights about two brothers who were trained by their father to hunt demons. At first, I was attracted to the program because of their car—a 1967 Chevy Impala. It took me back to my younger days when I would borrow a friend's 1964 Pontiac GTO and go cruising around the state park. God I loved that car. Sometimes he would even let me ride shotgun when he would drag race someone on the street. Now I'm really showing my age, huh? But as I further watched the tv series, it started to make some sense to me. I was (shall we say) learning. We don't know what to expect when the end of days happens and this program was giving me a possibility that it could really happen. Along with people more and more becoming used to the idea of ghosts, now we could start to make them more familiar with the idea of demons. Let's take us back to the days when religion was also a way of life. When as children we would also incorporate the Lord's prayer in our schoolday. When the word God was a part of The Pledge of Allegiance without controversy. We need to get back to the basics before it's too late!

I think it was the end of the third season in this particular tv program when Dean and Sam accidentally opened the door to Hell and released all the demons back out onto the earth. At the end of day's as we know it, why couldn't this be a possibility? Heaven and Hell will come together on the earth and do battle, this is a fact. The Bible tells us and men have preached this to us for all of time. Is this simple tv program trying to enlighten us to this fact while we watch worldly events unfold in our own modern day time? That we need to keep a watch out as more and more spirits and demons start to walk among us?

Anyway, I was finally released back to part time work by my doctor and I was hired at a combination pharmacy and convenience store located only three miles from our home. I was back to cashiering and loving it. Then I moved into what was called the courtesy window as bookkeeper and loved it even more. The managers were all great in the fact that sometimes I moved a little slower than others due to my back and it felt like being a part of another family. Life was good—accept for one thing.

It was six years that I stayed with that man. I loved him just about as much as Michael. My youngest daughter grew up knowing him as a stepfather even though we were never really married. My oldest daughter married his oldest son. My son told me that he considered him his father instead of his own birth-dad. We had a very good relationship, except for that one thing. This was eventually the cause for me to leave. Over the six years we stayed with him it showed it's ugly head enough times to erode the trust that I had in him. I won't mention what this problem is directly but believe me when I say that it has been the cause of many a breakup ever since the computer was allowed to be put into the hands of your average male.

To this day I do miss the life we had but when I left I put distance behind me. When I packed my car with as much as I could carry along with my youngest daughter, we didn't stop until we were six states away. My daughter asked me why we were leaving, even though she was all up on moving south she still wondered why. I thought about it a minute then explained that I had given her "stepfather" four chances and even in baseball you're considered out after three. That he had broke promises and trust and she seemed to accept this as explanation enough. But that I wouldn't ever keep her from communication with her real father or her grandmother up north.

Chapter VII

So I closed yet another chapter in my life and proceeded to try to make a living in a time when the economy was more than likely facing another depression. My mother was the reason why my youngest and I had the opportunity to move to Florida. Since way back in my younger days when my environmental allergy led to bronchitis and/or pnuemonia, then my back and then the arthritis, my doctor had been urging me for years to move somewhere to a warmer climate. Guess I finally listened huh? My latest ex-boyfriend and I had looked into the state of South Carolina to move to but I never could get him to take that leap.

I enrolled my daughter in a school that we both ended up liking. They taught math like it should be taught. Easy enough for me to understand so I could help teach her. Long division the right way. They were even willing to work with me on keeping her there in school should I move out of their district. Such an easy-going, friendly establishment they were.

It took me almost six months to find a steady income and just as long to find a reasonably priced place to live. At first, we moved into a dilapidated trailer which was all I could afford at the time. But at least it was a roof over our heads. The neighbors to the one side ended up being such fantastic people. They would do anything they could for us. But we were in an area that was on a county highway with no children around for my daughter to play with. Still this trailer seemed to be a good luck charm for us as it was here where I got hired to work for—guess what?—a behavioral center. That's right, as crazy as I am I fit right in. I was the receptionist. The one everybody saw first. Imagine that.

Our second residence was a two bedroom, two bathroom apartment in a low income housing complex. The apartment was beautiful and we were ecstatic to move in. But I soon came to realize that the environment was not really the best for my youngest. Her attitude took a turn for the worse.

It was also not a very good time for my oldest up north. Now keeping in mind that pestilence is one of the signs that we are warned of, bacteria has it's own way of changing to beat the antibiotics we produce to kill it. There had become a strain of strep (super-strep they call it) that was affecting young men and women in their teens that was killing them. I myself heard of four cases—my oldest daughter being one of them that contracted the virus. When I got the phone call informing me that she was going into surgery the next morning to fix her heart, I flew into a panic. The virus had spread throughout her body, shutting down her kidneys and infecting the valves in her heart. I couldn't get there! I couldn't console my daughter before she went under the knife! Later on that same day, she called me back and let me speak with the surgeon. In my fear and panic, I informed this poor man that he better not let my daughter die on his table. His response was that he was going to do everything in his power to not let that happen.

She went through the surgery extremely well and then I heard later on that afternoon that the surgeon had been the best in the entire world. I felt extremely humbled and wished I could have sent that man a dozen roses. Her husband never let a day go by without being there for her which most people would find admirable. However, not his employer. Like I said, I wasn't there to fully see the whole picture. But my daughter informed me that there had been no reason to lose his job over it as she wasn't going anywhere. Their marriage was on the rocks also and I guess he was just trying to fix it. She recuperated well and was released back to work after eight weeks.

I decided to start looking to buy my own house and get my youngest out of the conditions that were changing my daughter into a thug. But our lease wasn't going to be up before school ended and I drove my daughter back up north to spend the summer with her father and grandmother. On my return trip I brought my son down with me. I gave him fair warning that Florida wasn't in the greatest shape for trying to find work but he wanted to move down and give it a shot. My poor car—but it took it in great strides. Not just any car would have taken the miles I put on it—but my Lincoln did. I didn't know then just how many miles would go on my car before it did say "I give!" With me working full time hours (like I shouldn't have been doing) my son had no time to go look around for work himself. He did however use my computer to do the best that he could under the circumstances.

Then one day that August, I got a phone call from a very upset ex-boyfriend. It seemed there had been an accident that had ended up life-flighting his oldest son to the hospital. His son had been riding side-saddle on the back fender of the four-wheeler my ex-boyfriend had been driving and had fallen off when they came to a turn beside the road. Stumbling backwards, my oldest daughter's still husband had fallen and smacked his head hard enough on the pavement of the road to bounce him back up into a sitting position before slumping over sideways and laying lifeless on the berm of the road.

Now I believe that God takes care of his own. God works in mysterious ways as we all know. I'm sorry to say this but I believe that God took matters into his own hands. My daughter had once told me she believed her husband had been trying to kill her back before she had her heart surgery. He had loved her to a point of if I can't have you, no one can. She had been trying to file for divorce but could never afford it. Now here it was. They tried everything they could do, yet after ten days the family decided to pull the plug. He never regained consciousness. They had services in Ohio then cremated his body and transferred the ashes to his mother who now resided in New York where she could be closer to her mother and the Indian reservation. This incident broke the friendship of myself and my ex-boyfriend entirely.

I had become friends with the owner of a small computer shop in town when we first moved down who helped us so many times yet I found myself missing the days when I could be close to a man like Mark or Kenny. My trust in people was very limited. But then I have decided to stay pretty much to myself these days. You see if people outside of my immediate family heard some of the things I say now, they would commit me. Not even my own mother who lives just twenty minutes away from me accepts thoughts like ghosts, the end of the world, etc. She would call me by my name and say something like "You need help."

I have started to become aware of more fleeting shadows rushing by. Dreams more often than not affect me by night and day. I find myself talking to no one and yet feel the conversation in my head and comfort come over my body that lets me know someone is there. That's the best way to describe it. I guess maybe this has come about more so since that one day. Now I think I understand and that's why I'm telling you all this.

After my son moved down and my oldest daughter's husband passed away, I decided one day to get brave and do some research into finding where my old companions from Pennsylvania went to. Maybe it was the continuing comment of "Write it down" that kept coming into my head that helped to prompt this. It was something that kept at me every time I would have a free moment. Now if anyone knows the internet at all, you know that it can take a person forever to muddle around and maneuver yourself to the right places to find out almost anything. A lot of people finding places will tease you with the idea that they have the information as long as you will cough up your credit card numbers. This is probably true. But if you're anything like me, you don't have two red cents to rub together and come up with dinner money. So I went about locating him the around-about way.

When I started doing my search for Michael and his brother my fingers would start to almost hum and electrical charges would connect with my fingertips on the keyboard. Everytime I would start to type out their last name I would feel curiosity creep up inside me. This particular Saturday I was sitting at my kitchen table with my laptop and my son was watching tv on the couch in the living room thirty feet away from me.

First I was able to find out that he was still in Pennsylvania. They even had an address and phone number for him. Then I thought I found where his brother had moved to the same state as me.(This I think turned out to be false information). I started to get excited. Did I dare try to contact him after all these years? Should I contact his brother first? It had taken me weeks to decide to dig around and now trepidation was setting in. I forced myself to check for any old marriage announcements. There had to be more public information online for me to be able to get to. I found out where his father had an address listed. He had the same name as his father. So I decided to search out an obituary on his father. This man had been up there in age and you know how they'll list the relatives. That could tell me if Michael had ever married anyone. I went to the website for the local newspapers in that area and did a general search. Wouldn't you know it? As luck would have it, there was a listing from fifteen years prior involving the name. I went over to that newspaper's website and dug into the archives.

As the website took it's time to upload the article I was thinking "He lost his dad not long after I left the state. Right around the time I started having real trouble with my ex-husband."

When the article finally came up, I leaned forward to read the print. First was the full name followed by the age—36—then the explanation as to how the accident involving a gun had occurred killing the love of my life. He had been playing with it in a family hunting cabin with his companions when the gun went off shooting him in the head.

When what I was reading finally sank in, I suddenly felt like I had been punched in the stomach. I leaned backward so fast that I rocked the chair I had been sitting in I put my hands over my eyes and the words "Michael you dumbass!" blurted from my mouth. My son, startled, looked at me in shock. (My nephew has the same name) I explained it to him and he relaxed. But what came over me was the realization that I wouldn't be able to find him, wouldn't be able to call him, wouldn't be able to see him again on this earth!

As I sat there, I started to cry. Then I saw an image in my head of Michael standing behind me and reaching his arms around me to comfort me. I felt his arms around me and the tears wouldn't come. He had been there beside me trying to tell me all these years. Trying to reach out to me. It all made sense. The dreams, the visions, the once a year silent phone call on my birthday.

I walked around the next few weeks in shell shock. Almost everything put me into tears. I couldn't eat right. Here I was a middle-aged woman still in love with a man whom I always felt I would see again to finish out the relationship that never really ended. The man who I thought would always be there to go back to.

New songs on the radio seemed to reach out directly at me. One in particular comes to mind which talks about still missing someone no matter what you try to do or change. "But those old songs still sneak up" and remind you or how "after two drinks in and you're by my side". Another one tells the story of an old man who's always been waiting on a woman. Every time that video came on the tv I would imagine Michael up in heaven sitting on a bench dressed in blue jeans tapping his boots, smiling with his arm stretched out across the back of the park bench just waiting. This put me in tears every time. Thank you Brad for giving me some sense of peace. Another music video about a woman on her wedding day getting the letter delivered to her about her fiance being killed in battle and how her wedding day turned into the day of his funeral all hit so close to home as if I were transported back in time to the day of Michael's death. The songs seemed to be meant for me.

But the depression that stayed with me made me realize there was still a piece left undone. He wasn't yet quite in heaven. Hell, as I have said before, can be a personal one. He needed me to pull him from the depths of his own created hell to rise. I'm as good once as I ever was. With my son at work and my youngest at school one day, I walked into my bedroom and lit the candles that helped me to open the connection to my guardians and lifted him to the heavens above. Sounds nuts, don't it. But if you believe it, it will be.

Remember I told you I was trying to buy a house? Well that deal fell through but in the meantime my oldest daughter and her boyfriend moved down from Ohio and all of us lived in that house for the five months that it was ours. She flew me up to drive the moving van down and I made it a point that she retrieve my photo albums from her father-in-law's house. You see, Michael wouldn't let anybody take his picture. That is, except me. Back when Mark's apartment was the partying scene I had happened upon a disposable 3mm camera and focused on the man while he and Mark were sitting at Mark's kitchen table. They both saw me and Mark leaned out of frame laughing. Michael lifted one finger telling me to wait and placed two glassed under his high school football jersey that he could still wear, posed his right hand and smiling at me said, "Go". When Mark had the pictures developed, he brought them home before looking at them. Together we went through the pics and when I found the one of Michael I snagged it from him. Mark looked at me smiling and said, "I forgot all about that. You're lucky you took that, he never lets anybody take his picture." I held onto that picture all these years, I look at it every day.

When we moved out of the house I was trying to buy, I decided to move back to the original neighborhood where my youngest and I had lived in that very first dilapidated trailer. Now we were in a nice three bedroom, two bathroom trailer that has a full size kitchen, living room, screened room, back wooden deck and a laundry room.

When I pulled out Michael's picture to show my children who the love of my life was, they all fell silent. My oldest one looked at her brother and whispered something to him. Chuckling, he smiled and said, "Yeah, he does."

Curious I looked at them and said, "What?"

"He looks just like Shawn."

I looked back at the picture and saw what they were seeing. Michael had weighed about 230 lbs. where Shawn was a more slender 180 lbs. But they had had the same dark hair and eyes. The same skin color. The same neatly trimmed facial hair. They did resemble each other. Could Michael have used Shawn as an outlet? Would my youngest daughter have been Michael's if we had stayed together? Was it Michael who had spoken in my ear that one night I had conceived my youngest?

Since then I have felt his peace and love. Many nights we have met in my sleep. He has taken me to a place where he had wanted us to reside. Don't ask me where it was, I just let him lead. He is with me all the time. I am not alone and as I have told my children and mother, I am no longer afraid of dying. I know I have Michael on the other side waiting for me. Until then, I have things to do here. My body is my main concern right now. I can feel it almost getting ready to bust open and let God have this little piece back. For God no longer resides in Heaven. Nope, he's walking the earth right now. He looks around and he's worried. He sees the trouble we are all headed for and he sees Lucifer's work all around him. So He's getting ready to take back all the little pieces he's planted in each and every one of us—to ready for that last big battle before peace settles down on the earth. The seals the Bible speaks of are beginning to open and he cries at the devastation that he foresees. Even though time is only following his words, he still cries. He's still shocked that we didn't heed his words to avoid it. The armies are building readying for the battle. People like Sam and Dean and the rest of us are trying to save as many as we can. But then, this is what life is for. To teach, to save, to heal . . . all for the battle at the end of days.

I also have located my running buddy from Pennsylvania. Mark is currently living in South Carolina. Not far from the area where my ex-boyfriend and I were looking to move to that year before I moved to Florida. Ironic, isn't it? We're back in touch on the phone but I haven't made it up there yet to see how he's ended up doing.

I haven't been quite as successful locating Michael's brother. Maybe it wouldn't be such a good idea either though. I don't know who was in that hunting cabin with him but I wouldn't want to stir up bad memories either.

Now as I go through the rest of my life just waiting for the day when I can join him on that bench. I have no desire or want to meet anyone else. I know I have to bide my time until my number comes up in that great book. The day when I will open another chapter. Until then he will always be in my mind and my heart just as if he is beside me anyway. And I am his—Faithfully!